Graveyard Diaries

VAMPIRES ARE NOT YOUR FRIENDS

magic wagon

by Baron Specter
illustrated by Setch Kneupper

visit us at www.abdopublishing.com

Published by Magic Wagon, a division of the ABDO Group, PO Box 398166, Minneapolis, MN 55439. Copyright © 2013 by Abdo Consulting Group, Inc. International copyrights reserved in all countries. All rights reserved. No part of this book may be reproduced in any form without written permission from the publisher.

Calico Chapter Books™ is a trademark and logo of Magic Wagon.

Printed in the United States of America, North Mankato, Minnesota.
052012
092012
♻ This book contains at least 10% recycled materials.

Text by Baron Specter
Illustrations by Setch Kneupper
Edited by Stephanie Hedlund and Rochelle Baltzer
Interior layout and design by Neil Klinepier
Cover design by Neil Klinepier

Library of Congress Cataloging-in-Publication Data

Specter, Baron, 1957-
  Vampires are not your friends / by Baron Specter ; illustrated by Setch Kneupper.
      p. cm. -- (Graveyard diaries ; bk. 5)
  Summary: Mitch Morris really likes Mercy Knight, the new girl in Marshfield, but his friends are convinced that she and her parents are vampires.
  ISBN 978-1-61641-902-8
  1. Vampires--Juvenile fiction. 2. Haunted cemeteries--Juvenile fiction. [1. Vampires--Fiction. 2. Haunted places--Fiction. 3. Cemeteries--Fiction. 4. Mystery and detective stories.] I. Kneupper, Setch, ill. II. Title.
  PZ7.S741314Vam 2012
  813.6--dc23
                            2011052782

CONTENTS

Chapter 1:
The New Girl

Mitch's Notes: Wednesday, October 29. 4:10 p.m.

New girl in school today. Amy says she looks like trouble. I'll have to see about that.

Mitch Morris named his new document *Mitch's Notes*. He stared at the screen for a moment. Then he typed a few more words.

She just moved here. She kept asking me about the graveyards.

Mitch's mother looked into the den. "I'll need the computer in a few minutes," she said.

"Okay," Mitch said. "I was going out anyway." He typed one more line.

She said she liked getting scared sometimes.

Then he filed the document and logged off.

Something about the new girl was odd. She had told him her name—twice. But Mitch could not remember it.

Was it Mary? No. Mandy? Something like that. *Why can't I remember?* he wondered.

She had dark hair and her skin was pale. When she smiled, her dark brown eyes got wide.

Mitch left the house and walked right into Evergreen Cemetery. There were four cemeteries in the town of Marshfield.

Mitch and his friends lived on the edges of each one.

Mitch liked autumn. Many of the leaves had already fallen, but there were a lot of reds and yellows on the trees. Mitch kicked through some leaf piles on the dirt path.

He heard someone running through the leaves behind him. He turned to look. It was the new girl.

"Hi, Mitch!" she called.

"Hi," he said. "Um."

"It's Mercy," she said. "Did you forget my name already?"

"No!" Mitch said. "I just couldn't remember it."

"Isn't that the same as forgetting?"

Mitch kicked at the leaves. "I guess."

Mercy laughed. "I was out running. I love to run. This cemetery seems like a good place to do it."

"Yeah," Mitch said. "It's peaceful. No cars. Lots of birds and rabbits."

"Is it always peaceful?" she asked. "There must be ghosts. Aren't they in every graveyard?"

Mitch nodded. "Of course," he said.

Mitch had seen some strange things in this cemetery. Ghosts and other spirits. All four graveyards were haunted. Mitch and his friends often got together to talk about scary things they'd come across. They called their group the Zombie Hunters. They'd had some battles with evil spirits.

Mitch pointed toward a group of old gravestones under a big, dark tree.

"See those?" he said. "One night I was coming through here on my bike. It was about ten o'clock. I looked over there and got the scare of my life. Four ghosts were dancing on the graves. I could see them clearly."

"Did they see you?"

"I don't think so," Mitch said. "I was only eight, and I'd never seen a ghost before. And here were four of them. They were singing and floating and howling."

"Cool."

"It didn't seem cool at the time," Mitch said. "I didn't come near this place at night for months."

"But you do now?" Mercy said.

"Come out at night? Sure. All the time." Mitch folded his arms and looked around. "That was nothing. I see scarier stuff now."

"Sounds scary enough," Mercy said. "Why were you out here so late when you were eight years old?"

Mitch shrugged. "We were having a sleepover at my friend Barry's house. I didn't feel good. So I came home."

Mercy smiled. "I guess you wished you'd stayed at Barry's," she said.

"I guess," Mitch said. "But I would have seen a ghost sometime or another. There are lots of them around here."

When Mercy smiled, Mitch noticed that

she had some odd teeth. The front four looked fine, but the next ones were bigger than normal. They looked sharp.

Mercy saw Mitch looking. She shut her mouth tight. Then she said, "I'm going to get braces next year."

"Oh." Mitch looked down at the ground. He was sorry to have stared.

"The dentist says they'll be okay," Mercy said. "I'd love to come out here with you some night and see the spooks."

"You never know when you'll see one," Mitch said. "It's not a show."

"I know," Mercy said. "But don't forget what's coming this Friday—Halloween. I'll bet there will be lots of ghosts then."

"That's the night," Mitch said. "It's the one night of the year when you're almost certain to see them."

Mercy smiled again. "Please come out here with me then," she said. "My parents would never let me out here alone. And I don't know anyone else in town yet."

Mitch agreed. He and the other Zombie Hunters planned to be out that night anyway. One more person wouldn't hurt.

"We can come out here after the dance," Mercy said.

Mitch frowned. He knew about the school's sixth grade Halloween dance, but he didn't plan to go.

"I'm not going. The guys and I, we aren't

dancers," he said. "Maybe Amy would go. But the guys? No way."

"You don't have to dance," Mercy said. "We'll just kill time there. The dance ends at nine. It would be too early to come out here before that anyway."

"That's true," Mitch said.

"Dancing is fun," Mercy said.

"Maybe," Mitch said.

"What else are you going to do that night?" Mercy asked. "At least at the dance you can listen to music and drink free soda."

"I suppose," Mitch said.

"Great!" said Mercy. She started to run down the grassy hill. "See you at school," she called.

"Okay," Mitch replied. He stared at her until she was out of sight. Then, Mitch turned to walk home. Had he just been talked into going to the dance?

I must be losing my mind, he thought.

Chapter 2:
The Knights

Mitch's Notes: Wednesday, October 29. 6:45 p.m.

I have to get out of this stupid dance. The guys will never let me hear the end of it if I go. I'll come up with an excuse. I'll make up something to tell

Mitch stopped typing. He couldn't remember her name again! He typed *Mindy*. Then he erased that and typed *Misty*. Then he erased that and typed *her*.

I've got better things to do on Halloween than DANCE!

"Mitch!" his mom called from the kitchen. "Barry's here."

"Okay!" Mitch filed the document. He knew that Barry kept a diary about his adventures in the cemeteries. Mitch often teased Barry about it, but now Mitch was keeping one of his own.

This is different, Mitch thought. *This is a computer journal.*

But other than that, it didn't seem different.

"What's up?" Barry asked as Mitch entered the den.

"Not much," Mitch said. "I thought we were going to hang out at your house tonight. I was about to leave. I wanted to play your new video game."

"Okay," said Barry with a shrug. "Let's go."

Mitch put on a jacket and some gloves. The weather was cool and cloudy. They'd save time by cutting through the cemetery.

The boys headed out back. They walked along the same path Mitch had been on earlier.

"We haven't had a good scare lately," said Barry. "The ghosts and goblins have been quiet."

"I think that'll change soon," Mitch said. "Halloween is only two days away. And I have a weird feeling."

As they left the cemetery, Mitch heard someone call his name. Three people were coming out of the cemetery from a different path about thirty yards away.

"It's that new girl," Barry said.

Mercy waved as they walked over. "Meet my parents," she said. "Mr. and Mrs. Knight. This is Mitch. I met him at school today."

Mitch shook hands. Both of Mercy's parents had cold, bony hands. He introduced Barry.

The three Knights looked a little strange.

Mitch noticed that their lips were dark red and wet. Some of the color was dripping toward their chins.

Mitch looked closely at Mercy. Then he touched the corner of his own mouth. "You have something red there," he said.

"Oh," said Mercy. "We just ate pizza. A lot of it."

"At that place on Main Street," said Mr. Knight. He wiped his lips with the back of his hand.

"It was very saucy," said Mrs. Knight. She took out a handkerchief and wiped her lips, too. "We got it all over."

"Which place?" Mitch asked. There were three pizza parlors on Main Street.

"The small one," Mercy said.

"With the wooden tables," said Mr. Knight.

"And the spicy tomato sauce," said Mrs. Knight.

That described all three of the places. "I

see," said Mitch. "That might have been Leo's or Tony's."

"Or the Grotto," said Barry.

"It was one of those," Mercy said. "I forget the name." Mercy smiled.

Mitch noticed her sharp teeth again.

"I just remembered," said Mrs. Knight. "It was the Grotto."

"Yes," said Mr. Knight. "The Grotto. Such a nice place."

Mitch nodded. These people were odd.

"So, you boys go to school with Mercy?" said Mr. Knight.

"Yeah," said Mitch.

"She loves the school," said Mrs. Knight.

"After only one day?" Barry asked.

"Yes," said Mrs. Knight. "It's very friendly."

"And why are you here?" asked Mitch. He realized that he didn't sound very friendly. "I mean, it's great that you like our town. What brings you here?"

Mr. Knight smiled. He had the same dark hair as Mercy. Same pale skin, too.

"We're here for my work," said Mr. Knight. "It's a special project."

"Very special," said Mrs. Knight.

"For his work," added Mercy.

They all looked at each other for a moment. Finally Mercy broke the silence. "We'd better get going. I have math homework to do."

"There was no math homework today," Mitch said.

"I mean history," she said. The Knights walked away quickly.

Mitch watched them go. "There wasn't any history homework either," he said.

"Maybe she has a special project," Barry said. He laughed. "They didn't seem to be telling the truth."

"About what?"

"About anything," Barry said. "That wasn't pizza sauce on their lips. That was blood!"

Chapter 3:
Just Scared

Mitch's Notes: Thursday, October 30.   7:55 a.m.

Late for school. Have to hurry. I think Barry has watched too many horror movies. Or seen too many ghosts. The Knights are strange, but he thinks they're evil. I think he's imagining things.

At lunch, the Zombie Hunters sat together in a corner. Barry said he was definitely not going to any dance. Jared said he wouldn't go either. Stan said he wasn't sure.

"You guys are just scared," said Amy.

"We aren't scared of anything," said Barry. "I've faced ghosts and zombies and lots of other things in my life."

"And yet you're afraid to go to a dance," said Amy. "You're scared that you might actually like it."

Barry laughed. "Nothing scares me," he said. "What about you, Mitch? You haven't said a word."

"About what?"

"About the dance."

Mitch had been looking across the lunchroom. Mercy was sitting at a table with a few other kids. She seemed to make friends easily. He tried to see what she was eating. It was some kind of sandwich.

"Hey, Mitch," Barry said.

"What?"

"Are you going to the dance?"

Mitch shrugged. "I might. Just for laughs. I won't be dancing, that's for sure."

Amy looked over at Mercy. Then she

looked back at Mitch and smiled. "You might dance," she said. "Someone might talk you into it."

Barry put his fist down on the table. "This meeting is supposed to be about tomorrow night," he said. "Halloween. Ghost hunting. Not dancing."

Mitch cleared his throat. Barry always acted tough around other kids, but Mitch knew better. Barry liked to joke around. And he wrote poetry in his spare time. He wasn't so tough at all.

"I was thinking we should meet after nine o'clock," Mitch said. "Maybe we'll start in Evergreen and visit all four cemeteries."

"Sounds good," said Stan. "But why so late?"

Amy laughed. "Because the dance ends at nine."

"That has nothing to do with it," Mitch said. "Anything before that is too early for ghosts. They come out late."

"I'm going to bring a camera," Barry said. "Try to get some pictures of the ghosts."

"Good idea," said Stan. "I might do that, too."

Mitch looked across the lunchroom again. "One other thing . . . ," he said. "I told someone else it was okay to come with us."

"Who?" asked Barry. "This is supposed to be a Zombie Hunters' outing. Us only."

Mitch looked down at the table. He picked up a crust of bread from his tray. Then he set it down. "I got talked into it somehow," he said. "One more person won't hurt anything."

"Who is it?" Barry asked.

"I bet I know," said Amy.

Mitch frowned. "She'll be okay," he said. He blushed.

Barry shook his head. "The girl with the

bloody mouth?"

"She seems cool to me," Mitch said. "I think she might make a good Zombie Hunter."

"She might," Amy said. "But I'd be careful around her."

"Why?" Mitch asked.

"Something about her isn't right," Amy said.

"Get out," said Mitch. "You guys are imagining things."

The bell rang for the end of the lunch period. The Zombie Hunters headed for their classrooms.

Mitch felt a tug on his arm as he was walking out.

"Hi, Mitch," said Mercy. She had a big smile on her face.

"Oh . . . hi."

"I'm so excited about the dance tomorrow," she said. "Aren't you?"

Mitch rolled his eyes. "Not exactly," he

said.

"It will be fun," Mercy said. "You'll see. What time are you going to pick me up?"

Mitch stopped walking. "I thought we'd just meet at the dance."

"No," she said. "Come by my house about six forty-five. We'll have some Halloween candy."

Mitch couldn't think of an excuse. "Okay," he said.

Mercy told him the address. "What are you wearing?" she asked.

Mitch looked down at his jeans. He pulled on the front of his shirt. "Something like this," he said.

Mercy laughed. "It's a Halloween dance!" she said. "You're supposed to wear a costume."

"Oh." Mitch was twelve years old. It had been a couple of years since he'd dressed up for Halloween.

"I'll find something," he said. He was

sure some of his old masks were in a closet. But this was shaping up to be more than he expected.

"Thanks again for inviting me," Mercy said. "I'll see you later." She hurried away.

"You're welcome," Mitch replied.

But I didn't invite her to go anywhere, he thought.

Chapter 4:
Mitch's Place

Mitch's Notes: Thursday, October 30. 4:06 p.m.

I need a long walk in the cemetery to clear my head. Mercy is twisting me around. She talks me into things that I don't want to do. At least, I don't think I want to do them. Like the dance. Or picking her up at her house. Why can't we just skip the whole thing?

The afternoon was warm and clear. Mitch headed to his favorite part of the cemetery. He climbed a steep hill. The trees up here were mostly pines. The path was rough and full of rocks.

Mitch came to a small clearing. This was the oldest part of the cemetery. Very few people ever visited this spot anymore. Most of the graves were more than 200 years old.

Mitch sat on a large rock. The sun felt good on his face. All around him was a thick forest, but this spot was open. There were about a dozen gravestones here. Most of the last names on the stones were Chase or Duncan.

One night last summer, Mitch and Barry had pitched a tent on this hill. Around midnight, they heard people singing. The song was slow and sad.

They crept out of the tent and moved very slowly toward the sound. They saw several ghostly figures standing near a grave. Some were children. Mitch and Barry could see right through them.

It was scary, but the ghosts seemed peaceful. Mitch and Barry watched for a long time. Then they went back to the tent. The ghosts didn't seem to be aware of them.

Mitch had never felt much danger in Evergreen Cemetery. He'd had some rough times in the town's other graveyards. Especially with the other Zombie Hunters. But so far, every ghost he'd seen in Evergreen had minded its own business.

Mitch picked up a pebble and tossed it at a pine tree. There weren't many bright leaves up here. The maple trees were in the lower areas.

Mitch had friends who were girls. Amy was clever and a great member of the Zombie Hunters. He liked to joke around with her. But Mercy seemed interested in Mitch in a different way. And he was starting to think that he felt that way, too. Maybe the dance would be fun after all.

He stepped over to one of the gravestones.

JOHN CHASE
BORN JANUARY 15, 1798
DIED MARCH 21, 1809
AT PEACE

"Eleven years old. Just a year younger than me," Mitch said. He looked at the thin granite stone. The letters were faded. There was a large crack that went right through John's name. Pale green lichen covered part of the stone.

Mitch wondered when John Chase last had a visitor. The most recent gravestone he could find in this spot was from 1830. Was that the last of John's family? Had he been forgotten for all this time?

"I'll visit you," Mitch said, patting the top of the stone. He liked the idea that this spot was nearly John's alone.

Maybe I'll show these gravestones to Mercy, he thought. *She'd like this place.*

A sound in the forest made Mitch look up. Something was running. A squirrel ran up a tree and stopped, looking back at Mitch.

"Nothing scary here," Mitch said. "Not today."

Tomorrow night might be different. Halloween was the most active night of all for ghosts. But Mitch didn't want to stir up any trouble here in Evergreen. Maybe visiting the other three graveyards would be enough. This place was special. He felt like it was his own.

Mitch sat on the rock again and felt the warmth on his face. He stayed there until the sun had set behind the hill.

Barry and Jared would give him a hard time about going to the dance. But so what? Amy was going. Stan probably would, too.

And later, they'd all have a spooky time in the graveyards.

Chapter 5:
Missing Blood

Mitch's Notes: Thursday, October 30. 5:48 p.m.

I tried to dance. I shut my bedroom door and put on some music. Then I stood in front of the mirror. I looked so stupid that even I had to laugh. Imagine what I'd look like at the dance!

B arry rang the doorbell while Mitch and his family were eating dinner.

"Can he wait in my room?" Mitch asked his parents.

"Sure," said his mom.

"We're almost done," Mitch said. Barry

looked like he needed to talk.

Mitch finished eating and asked to be excused.

"Did you read the newspaper today?" Barry asked as soon as Mitch closed his bedroom door.

"Not yet."   The town's weekly newspaper arrived every Thursday. Mitch always read the sports section.

"Look at this," Barry said. He pointed to an article on the front page. The headline said "Missing Blood." The article read:

At least ten pints of blood are missing from last week's blood drive. The Red Cross collected 209 pints of blood from volunteers on Friday. But fewer than 200 of those pints made it to the blood bank. Marshfield Police are investigating.

"That's a shame," Mitch said. "So?"

"That's where they got the blood!" Barry said.

"Who?"

"That girl and her parents," Barry said. "The ones we saw last night with blood all over their mouths."

Mitch thought about that for a moment. "Why would they do that?" he finally asked.

"Because they're vampires," Barry said. "Don't you see?"

"Mercy's not a vampire," Mitch said. "They can't be out in daylight."

"I don't think that's true," Barry said. "I read somewhere that they just made that up for the movies."

"Let's look it up," Mitch said. They went downstairs to use the computer.

Barry was right. Vampires had been reported for centuries. But the idea that they couldn't be out during the day was new. It had first been suggested in a horror

movie. That was less than 100 years ago.

"See?" Barry said. "Real vampires can be out anytime."

"That doesn't mean that Mercy is one," Mitch said.

"What about her fangs?" Barry said.

"The dentist is going to fix them."

"But why are they like that?" Barry asked. "So big and sharp."

"They aren't fangs!" Mitch said. He pointed to his own side teeth. "Look.

Everybody has sharp teeth there. Hers are just a little sharper, that's all."

Barry shook his head and laughed. "You have a crush on her, don't you?"

"No."

"You do."

Mitch closed the screen, making the vampire Web site disappear. "Shut up about that," he whispered. He pointed his thumb toward the kitchen. "My parents are right there."

Barry nodded. They climbed the stairs to Mitch's room again.

"You're going to that dance with her?" Barry asked.

"Not just with her," Mitch said. "Amy and Stan are going. It's no big deal."

"Just watch out," Barry said. "If she bites you, you might get infected."

"She won't bite me."

"If you get bit by a vampire you'll become one, too," Barry said.

"I won't get bit. And she's not a vampire."

But Mitch wasn't really sure. *I hope she's not,* he thought. *That would make it tough to have her as a friend.*

"Don't dance too close," Barry said.

"I won't be dancing at all," Mitch said. "I told you, I'm just going to the dance for laughs."

"You won't be laughing much if she bites you," Barry said. "If that happens, you'll be the one drinking blood from the Red Cross."

"One bite doesn't turn you into a vampire," Mitch said.

"It could."

"No, it couldn't," Mitch said. "That's a myth."

"Not always," Barry said. "I'd carry some garlic if I were you."

"To the dance?"

"Yeah," Barry said. "Any time you're

with her. Garlic keeps vampires away."

"What if I don't want her to stay away?" Mitch said.

"Bring the garlic."

"I'm not bringing garlic," Mitch said. "It stinks."

"That's the idea," Barry said. "The smell keeps them away."

"She's not a vampire," Mitch said.

At least he was pretty sure that she wasn't.

Chapter 6:
The Monster Mash

Mitch's Notes: Friday, October 31. 6:30 p.m.

I'm leaving for the dance in five minutes. To watch the dance. There's no way I'll actually be dancing. Just killing time until the real fun starts. Halloween is here! Can't wait to visit the graveyards.

Mitch put on a football jersey. He took the gorilla mask from his closet. It wasn't a very clever costume, but it would do.

On the way to Mercy's house, he passed groups of trick-or-treaters. He'd loved to do that when he was little. The best part was walking through the cemetery at night. It was scary, but it felt peaceful. He knew that Halloween was a special night for hauntings.

There were three jack-o'-lanterns on the Knights' porch. Mercy answered the door with a big smile. She was wearing a black outfit with a long tail and cat ears. Around her neck was a thin, black necklace with a pale blue stone.

"Come in!" she said. "We were just having a snack."

Mr. and Mrs. Knight were in the kitchen. They each had a glass of dark red liquid.

"Can Mitch have some?" Mercy asked.

"Sorry," said Mr. Knight. "This was the last of it."

"It's all gone," said Mrs. Knight. "Would you like some Halloween candy instead?" She held out a bowl of candy.

"Thanks," said Mitch. He took off his

gorilla mask and grabbed a chocolate bar.

"Let's go," Mercy said. She turned to her parents. "I'll be home after ten. Okay?"

"Okay," said Mr. Knight. "Have fun."

They hurried down the walk toward school.

"Sorry we ran out of juice," Mercy said.

"That's okay," Mitch said. "What kind of juice was that?"

"A mix," Mercy replied. "Tomatoes and berries. And beets, I think. Red things."

"I see."

"It's for grown-ups," Mercy said. "My parents let me taste it a few days ago. It's supposed to be very good for you."

"Oh."

"My parents say it's their life force," Mercy said with a laugh. "It has lots of vitamins, I guess. But it tasted salty."

Mitch wondered what was really in the juice. It looked like blood to him. Was Barry right?

"Where did you come from?" Mitch asked.

"We were living in New Jersey for a while," Mercy said. "But we move around a lot because of my father's work."

Mitch nodded. New Jersey was a long way from Marshfield.

"I'm hoping we can finally settle down here," Mercy said. "I'm tired of having to make new friends all the time."

They could hear the music as they reached the school. The band was playing an old rock-and-roll song.

"Sounds great!" Mercy said. "Let's get inside."

The gym was filled with kids, but very few were dancing. The band on the stage had a drummer and two guitarists. The overhead lights were turned off. Some red and blue lights were shining from near the stage.

Mitch looked around for Stan. He finally

found him sitting in a folding chair off to the side near some other guys.

Amy was dancing with a group of girls. Mercy rushed out to join them.

"Having fun yet?" Mitch asked Stan. Stan was wearing makeup that made him look like a zombie. He had a cup of soda.

Stan frowned. "It's okay, I guess," he said. "You haven't missed anything."

Mitch took off his mask again. It was making him sweat. "No boys are dancing I see."

"No," Stan said. "Nobody wants to be the first one."

"I don't even want to be the last one," Mitch said. But he started tapping his feet when the band played "Light My Fire." The girls seemed to be having a lot of fun.

After a few more songs, Amy and Mercy came over.

"You're missing a great time," Amy said.

"We're watching," Mitch said.

"That's not the same," Mercy said. "You should get up and dance."

Mitch looked down at his feet.

"Let's get some food," Amy said.

A table was set up near the back of the gym. There was free soda, cookies, and pizza. Mitch picked up a slice of pizza.

"It's from the Grotto," he said. He held the slice out to Mercy. "Want some?"

Mercy smiled, but she shook her head. "I can't have pizza," she said. "There's too much garlic in the sauce."

"You can't eat garlic?"

"I'm allergic to it," Mercy said. "My parents are, too. It runs in the family."

Mitch looked at the pizza, then at Mercy. Vampires had to avoid garlic. Something wasn't adding up here.

"I thought you had pizza at the Grotto a few nights ago," he said.

"Oh." Mercy put her hand to her mouth. She didn't say anything for a few seconds.

"I forgot," she said. "I mean, we forgot that we were allergic. To garlic."

Mitch didn't believe that. "So, did you get sick?"

"No," Mercy said. "We didn't eat very much."

"I guess you remembered about the garlic all of a sudden," Mitch said.

"Yeah," Mercy replied. "So, let's dance some more."

Mitch took a step back. "Not me."

"But you promised that you would," Mercy said.

"No, I didn't."

"Sure you did."

Mitch looked at Stan. Both boys laughed. "No, I didn't," Mitch said again.

"Let's flip a coin," Mercy said. "If it's heads, you have to dance with me. If it's tails, I have to dance with you."

"Ha!" Mitch said. "Some deal."

"It's easy," Amy said. "Come on, you

guys. Don't be spoilsports."

Mitch looked at Stan. Stan shrugged.

"Don't say a word about this to Barry and Jared," Mitch said.

"About what?" Stan asked.

"You know," Mitch replied. He led the way back to the chairs so he could get his mask. At least the gorilla face would give him some cover.

The band started to play "Monster Mash."

Mercy and Amy clapped as the boys stepped onto the floor with them. Mitch tried to do the same as Mercy, just swinging his arms a little in time to the music. He moved his shoulders around, too.

Mercy was grinning and her eyes were sparkling. She pointed to her feet. She took a soft step out with her right foot, then her left. Then she stepped back in. She repeated that motion over and over.

Mitch tried to do the same. He felt

awkward and silly. But then he noticed that several other boys were dancing, too. He and Stan had been the first.

"Good," Mercy said. She pointed to Mitch's feet. "Out, out. In, in."

When the song ended, Mercy patted Mitch's arm. "You were great!" she said. But she was laughing.

Mitch didn't care. He knew he didn't dance very well. But Mercy was fun to be with, even if she didn't always tell the truth.

They danced to a few more songs. When the band played a slow one, Mitch smiled and walked off.

They all sat down. A few couples were dancing slowly. Mitch felt a little strange. He didn't look at Mercy.

"I'm hungry," Mercy said. "Let's get some cookies."

A little later Mitch danced with Mercy again. He kept his mask on, but he didn't really care if anyone was watching.

When the dance ended, Mitch took off the mask. Stan said he needed to go home for his camera and a flashlight. Amy went with him since they were neighbors.

"Meet you at the entrance to Evergreen in twenty minutes," Stan said.

So Mitch and Mercy walked toward the cemetery. Barry and Jared were supposed to be there at nine fifteen.

"Thank you for taking me to the dance," Mercy said. "It was so much fun."

"It was," Mitch said. It had been a lot more fun than he'd expected.

"Do you think we can see those dancing ghosts you told me about?" Mercy asked.

"We can try." It had been several years since Mitch had seen them.

Mitch and Mercy walked along the path into Evergreen Cemetery. They kicked fallen leaves as they went.

There was no sign of the ghosts.

"Maybe later," Mitch said. "It's still pretty early."

The moon was up, but the graveyard was quite dark. Mercy leaned her shoulder against Mitch. He leaned back. She turned her head and looked up at him.

Mitch could see those sharp teeth. Mercy leaned closer. Her breath smelled like peppermint. She brought her lips close to his neck.

"Hey, Mitch!" somebody yelled.

Mitch and Mercy stepped back. Jared and Barry were walking toward them, shining their flashlights.

"What are you doing?" Barry asked. "We were supposed to meet at the entrance."

"We were looking for ghosts," Mitch said.

Barry sneered. He glanced at Mercy. "Find any?" he asked.

"Not yet," Mitch said. "We just got here."

Barry reached over and pulled back the collar of Mitch's shirt.

"What are you doing?" Mitch asked. He pushed Barry's hand away.

"Checking for fang marks," Barry said.

Mitch smacked Barry's arm. "Get lost," he said.

They started walking back toward the entrance. Mitch looked at Mercy. She raised her eyebrows and smiled.

Mitch felt his neck, just to be sure. Mercy hadn't bit him. But had she been about to when Barry interrupted them?

Or was Mitch just imagining things?

Chapter 7:
Crashing a Funeral

"So what's the plan?" Mitch asked as the Zombie Hunters gathered at the entrance to Evergreen Cemetery.

"Who's seen any ghosts lately?" Barry asked. "Which cemetery is hot?"

Since each of them lived at the edge of a graveyard, they gave reports. Mitch said Evergreen had been quiet. Barry said Marshfield Grove was, too.

"I've heard some things at night by Woodland," Jared said. "Just some spooky voices. Nothing too scary."

"Same at Hilltop," said Stan. "As far as I know." He looked at Amy, who lived less than a block away from him.

"I think the spirits have been resting," Amy said. "But they'll wake up tonight."

"Then let's start here," Barry said. "Mitch and Mercy did some checking for ghosts already. Or were you two doing something else?"

"Like what?" Mitch asked.

Barry made kissing sounds. The others all laughed.

"Knock it off," Mitch said. He gave Barry a light shove. Then he blushed.

"So where to?" Jared asked.

"I visited a cool spot yesterday," Mitch said. "Up the hill. Remember, Barry? We saw ghosts there last summer."

"Right. They were singing hymns," Barry said. "Okay. Let's head there."

They walked a few feet. Then Barry stopped. "Remember," he said, "be quiet and respectful. We don't want to disturb the ghosts—just watch them."

Mitch walked next to Mercy. When they reached the hill, she leaned toward him. She made a kissing sound like Barry had. Then she laughed.

"Quiet back there," Barry said in a loud whisper.

Mitch looked at Mercy. She stuck out her tongue toward Barry. Then she smiled.

When they reached the grave site, they spread out and found places to sit. Mitch and Mercy leaned against a boulder. The night was clear and cool. There was a light wind.

"Right over there," Mitch said softly, pointing toward the gravestones. "There were at least six ghosts one night last summer. I think they were having a funeral."

"Creepy," Mercy said. "Who died?"

Mitch smirked. "All of them," he said.

They watched for a long time. Mitch thought he saw some movement, but no ghosts appeared. *Just the breeze,* he decided.

And then he saw a flicker of light. It floated above one of the graves. It wasn't very bright. It had a soft green tint.

Mitch gripped Mercy's arm. "There," he whispered. "You see it?"

Mercy nodded. She was staring hard.

Two more lights appeared. All three took the form of people. One was a little girl. The other two looked like adults. They were misty, so it was hard to tell.

Soon there were three more ghosts. They stayed by one grave. Mitch could see that it was John Chase's. Was this his funeral?

Mitch leaned forward. He strained to hear. The ghosts were singing. It was the same sad song he'd heard last summer.

One of the ghosts began reading from a book. It looked like a Bible. Mitch could

only hear a few of the words. But he did hear the name John.

"That boy was eleven when he died more than 200 years ago," Mitch whispered.

"Wow," Mercy said. "Why would they still be having his funeral?"

"I have no idea," Mitch said. "Ghosts are hard to figure out."

The ghosts sang another song. But then there was a clicking sound and a flash of light. The ghosts stopped singing and vanished.

"What happened?" Mitch said. He saw Barry walking toward the grave with his camera.

"Why did you take a picture now?" Mitch asked. "We said we wouldn't disturb them."

"Sorry," Barry said. "I didn't think they'd notice."

Jared, Stan, and Amy walked over, too.

"That was very cool," Amy said. "Too

bad you scared them off, Barry."

Barry shrugged. "Yeah, but I've got the shot of a lifetime right here." He held up the camera and looked at it. "Can't see much now. I'll check it out at home later."

"I hope you didn't make them mad," Mitch said. "You never know what a ghost might do. Especially when you interrupt a funeral!"

Mitch walked to the grave. He shined his light along the ground. There was no sign that anyone had been there. Ghosts don't leave footprints.

"Two hundred years," Stan said. "That's a long time ago."

"Why do the ghosts keep having his funeral?" Amy asked.

"Maybe because he's not a ghost," Mitch said. "Maybe they're hoping he'll join them."

"Yeah," Barry said. "Not everybody becomes a ghost."

"Where to next?" Mitch asked.

"Marshfield Grove is closest," Barry said. "Let's go there."

They started to walk, but then they heard a laugh. It came from the bottom of the hill. Then there were footsteps and an eerie voice.

Someone was approaching very slowly. Mitch gripped his flashlight and waited.

Whoever it was, he or she was coming up the hill toward them.

Chapter 8:
Once Bitten

Mitch and the others backed slowly into the woods. It sounded like two adults were coming up the hill. They were giggling.

When they came into sight, Mercy gasped. "It's my parents," she whispered.

Mr. Knight was carrying a bottle. By the light of the moon, Mitch could see that it probably held that "juice."

"I thought they ran out of that," he said to Mercy.

"I guess they found some more," Mercy said.

Mr. and Mrs. Knight walked by slowly. They both took sips from the bottle. Their mouths were dark red.

The kids stayed very still until the adults had left the area.

"Now that was creepy," Barry said.

"Why was it creepy?" Mercy asked. "They were just out for a walk."

"In the cemetery?" Barry said. "In the dark? And that wasn't lemonade they were drinking."

"It's a special juice," Mercy said.

"It's stolen blood!"

Mercy shook her head. "No, it isn't."

"They're vampires," Barry said.

"They are not!" Mercy said. "Don't be so mean."

Mitch stepped between Barry and Mercy. "Leave her alone," he said.

"I'm not picking on her," Barry said. "I'm talking about her parents."

"Well, stop it," Mitch said. "You don't know what they were drinking."

"It was blood," Barry said. "And you'd better watch yourself, Mitch. She must be a vampire, too."

"That's a horrible thing to say," Mercy replied. "You don't know what you're talking about."

"Shut up, Barry," Mitch said.

Mercy was crying. Amy patted her shoulder. "It's okay," Amy said. "Boys can be jerks."

They began walking again. Mitch walked slowly next to Mercy. They let the others get far ahead.

"I don't want to hang out with them tonight," Mercy said. "Barry was really awful to say that."

Mitch nodded. But he was afraid that Barry was right. Mr. and Mrs. Knight did seem like vampires. But what about Mercy?

"Do you think those ghosts will come back tonight?" Mercy asked.

"The funeral ones? Maybe."

Mercy stopped walking. "Can we go back and see?"

"If you want to," Mitch said.

"I do."

They turned around. Mitch felt bad for Mercy. "Don't worry about what Barry said."

"It wasn't very nice," Mercy said.

They climbed the hill and leaned against the same boulder.

"My parents are good people," Mercy said.

"They seem nice."

"They'd never hurt anyone," Mercy said.

Mitch nodded. He folded his arms and looked up at the trees.

"I'm not a vampire!" Mercy said. "You believe me, don't you?"

"I'm here with you, aren't I?" Mitch said.

"Yes, you are." Mercy reached over and squeezed Mitch's arm. "Thanks for being so nice to me."

"You too," Mitch said. He was glad she had talked him into going to the dance. He never would have done that before.

"Look," Mercy said softly. She pointed toward the grave. The ghosts had gathered again. They were standing in a circle.

Mitch put a finger to his lips. "Quiet now," he said.

The ghosts seemed to be starting the funeral all over again. They sang the same song. Then one of the men read from the Bible.

"Do you think they do this every night?" Mercy asked.

"Maybe," Mitch said. "Ghosts usually repeat things over and over. They get stuck."

"That's kind of sad," Mercy said. "But kind of sweet, too."

When the ghosts were finally gone, Mitch stood up. He reached out his hand to help Mercy to her feet. Her hand was very cold.

"Why are ghosts like that?" Mercy asked. "Doing the same thing every night."

"They're spirits that can't get free," Mitch said. "Something happened when they were alive that they can't recover from. So they keep replaying it to try to get it right."

"How could a funeral go wrong?" Mercy asked.

"I don't think it's that," Mitch said. "I think they can't get over losing that kid. John Chase. It must have been really sad when he died so young."

"I see."

"Certain things can just stay with you," Mitch said. "Some people spend a lifetime trying to get over them."

"Or a lot longer," Mercy replied. "Like 200 years."

"You said it."

It was after ten o'clock. They couldn't stay out much longer. But Mitch didn't want the evening to end. He liked talking to Mercy.

They walked toward Main Street.

"Are you really allergic to garlic?" Mitch asked.

"I don't know," Mercy said. "My parents said we should avoid it. I don't know why."

"But you said you all ate that pizza a few nights ago."

"I did?"

"Yeah," Mitch said. "When we met at the edge of the cemetery."

"Oh, yeah."

"So what was all over your mouth?" Mitch asked. "That juice?"

Mercy shrugged. They'd reached Main Street. She took a seat on a bench. Mitch sat next to her.

"My parents told me not to say anything about the juice," Mercy said. "I think it's their special recipe. They want to try to sell it. So they don't want anyone to steal the idea."

"Oh."

"Even I don't know exactly what's in it," Mercy said. "Like I told you, red things like berries."

Mitch watched two cars and a pickup truck drive by. "I'll bet it's very tasty," he finally said.

"You don't sound convinced."

"I don't know," Mitch said. "It seems a little doubtful."

"Oh, come on," Mercy said. "You don't

believe what Barry said, do you?"

Mitch shook his head. "Of course not." But that was a lie. And if Mercy's parents were vampires, then wouldn't she be one, too?

"They're odd," Mercy said. "I don't deny that. But they're very good people."

That seemed to be the truth.

"I should get home," Mercy said. "It's late."

Mitch stood up. He took Mercy's hand to help her up.

They didn't say much as they walked toward Mercy's house. They stopped at the end of her driveway.

"That was a great night," Mercy said. "I hope we stay in this town."

"I hope so, too," Mitch said.

Mercy lifted his hand and gave it a light kiss. But then Mitch felt something hard and sharp on his hand, like a pinch.

Mitch pulled away. "Did you just bite

my hand?" he asked.

Mercy smiled. "Not really," she said.

Mitch looked at his hand. There was a small mark below his knuckles. But the skin wasn't broken.

Mercy took his hand and rubbed it between hers. "Sorry," she said. "I didn't hurt you, did I?'

"No . . . ," Mitch said.

"I don't know why I did that," Mercy said.

"It's okay," Mitch said. "It tickled."

Mercy laughed. "Well, good night," she said. She went up the walk and into the house.

Mitch turned and started running. He had a lot of energy. He stayed on the dark back streets. He ran for about fifteen minutes.

He was happy. He was excited. But one thought kept running through his mind.

Did I just get infected by a vampire?

Chapter 9:
Bad Breath

As soon as he got home, Mitch went to the kitchen. He opened the refrigerator. In the produce drawer, he found what he needed—a fresh bulb of garlic.

He didn't know how much to eat. But if garlic kept vampires away, would it also keep him from being infected? Even after being bitten?

He peeled off two cloves. He popped them into his mouth and chewed. The garlic had a very strong taste. He chewed it up good and swallowed.

"Yuck," he said. He took a big gulp of orange juice to try to kill the taste. But it didn't work.

He went to the den and turned on a lamp. He took a close look at the back of his hand under the light. There were two tiny marks from Mercy's teeth. But no blood.

Mitch let out a sigh of relief. But he wanted to make sure he was safe.

He knew that there were a lot of Web sites about vampires. He'd looked at many of the sites before. Some were silly. He searched for one that had solid information. He needed to know what else to do after being bitten.

"Drink the ashes of a burnt vampire." Mitch winced. He wouldn't be doing that!

"Hang a bag of salt around your neck." He could do that. But how much? He went to the kitchen and shook some salt into a handkerchief. He tied it into a tight bundle. Then he tied a shoelace around the bundle and hung it like a necklace. The salt rested against his chest.

There were other suggestions, but Mitch had no way to try them. "Mix the blood of a dead vampire with flour and bake it into bread. Then eat it." He shook his head.

He felt for the bundle of salt. *This should be enough,* he thought. *Especially since there was no blood.*

Mitch's Notes: Friday, October 31. 11:37 p.m.

Halloween has been great! Mercy is really something. I like to hang out with her. I'm not so sure about her parents, though. They seem to drink a lot of blood. Maybe Mercy is too young to be a vampire. But she does act a little bit like one.

Mitch went to another Web site. He learned a few new things about vampires. They drank blood to absorb the strength of their victims. And bitten victims didn't always turn into vampires.

An instant message popped onto his screen. It was from Barry.

Barry: Hey, dude! Almost midnight. Can you get out?

Mitch stayed still for a moment. The upstairs of the house was dark. He hadn't heard anything from up there. His parents must be asleep.

He responded to the message.

Mitch: Yes. Where?

Barry: The chapel.

The chapel was in the Marshfield Grove cemetery. It was near Barry's house. They'd seen some very spooky things there. Midnight on Halloween should be a busy time for ghosts.

Mitch put on a warm sweatshirt and a

jacket. He wanted to brush his teeth, but that might disturb his parents. So he took another drink of orange juice. His mouth still tasted awful.

I guess that's a good thing, he thought. The garlic would make sure there was no infection.

Mitch carefully opened the front door and slipped out. He touched the top of the pumpkin on the porch for good luck. He'd carved a smiling face in it a few days ago.

Then he ran all the way to Marshfield Grove. He seemed to have extra energy tonight. Maybe from all those cookies at the dance.

Barry was waiting by the chapel. It was up on a hill in a dark corner of the cemetery. The chapel was small and made of stones. The windows were boarded up. No one had used the chapel for many years.

There were several graves behind the chapel. Mitch and Barry had been there a lot at night. They often saw ghosts.

"What happened to you?" Barry said. "You disappeared earlier."

"We went back to watch the funeral again," Mitch said.

"Why didn't you stay with us?" Barry asked.

"Because you weren't being nice to Mercy."

Barry shrugged. "I was just telling the truth. I'll bet her parents stole that blood."

"I could have punched you."

Barry held up the palms of his hands. "Whoa," he said. "It wasn't that bad."

"It wasn't cool," Mitch said. "She's really nice. Don't pick on her."

Barry sat down on a low wall by the chapel. "Okay," he said. "I'm sorry."

"Don't tell me."

"I'll tell her next time I see her," Barry said. "Deal?"

"Okay."

They watched the graves for a while, but nothing happened.

"Did she bite you?" Barry asked.

Mitch shook his head. "Not really."

"What do you mean?" Barry replied. "Either she did or she didn't."

Mitch turned on his flashlight. He held it above his hand. Barry leaned over to examine the teeth marks.

"Wow!" Barry said. "You stink!"

"I ate some garlic."

Barry put his hand over his nose. "How much did you eat? Ten pounds?"

"Two little cloves," Mitch said. "Do I really smell that bad?"

"Gross!" But Barry leaned closer to look at Mitch's hand. "Doesn't look like much," he said. "But next time might be worse."

"She won't bite me again," Mitch said.

"They can't control it!" Barry said. "Vampires need blood. And she seems to want yours."

Mitch let out a big sigh. "Maybe," he said. "But I'll be careful."

"Don't worry," Barry said with a laugh. "With that garlic smell, she won't want to get anywhere near you for a while."

"I'll buy some breath mints," Mitch said. He didn't want to stay away from Mercy.

Barry stood up. "Nothing going on here," he said. "The ghosts must be someplace else."

"Let's go back to Evergreen," Mitch said. "There's bound to be action there."

He looked at his watch. It was exactly midnight.

And suddenly he heard voices from the chapel!

Chapter 10:
A Real Halloween Dance

Mitch stood on tiptoe and peered through a hole in one of the boards. He could see several ghosts in the chapel. A soft song was coming from a flute.

The ghosts began to dance. It looked sort of like a waltz. The music was very pleasant. Mitch moved to another window to try to get a better look.

"Over here," Barry called.

Barry was at the front door. There was a large opening in the wood there. Mitch joined him.

Mitch froze as the door began to open. He was face-to-face with a ghostly woman. She waved at the boys to come in.

Mitch looked at Barry. They both laughed nervously. Then they stepped into the chapel.

Ten ghosts were dancing. Another ghost was playing a fiddle and another was playing a flute. Mitch and Barry stayed close to the door.

"Cool," Barry whispered.

"You got to a Halloween dance after all," Mitch said.

The ghost who had let them in floated over. Another woman was with her. They held out their hands to the boys.

"You want us to dance?" Barry asked.

The women nodded.

Mitch gulped. He took a step forward. *This is crazy,* he thought.

Barry looked frozen. He didn't move at all. Mitch touched his arm. He pointed to

his own feet and did the steps Mercy had shown him. Right foot out a little. Left foot out a little. Then back in. Over and over.

Barry tried, too. "We're dancing with ghosts!" he said.

"Shhh," Mitch said. "They don't know they're dead."

They danced until the end of the song. Mitch was sweating, but he was shivering. Barry backed up against the wall again.

The women bowed and went back across the room. Mitch stood next to Barry and watched the dancing ghosts.

"Can you believe this?" Barry whispered.

Mitch just shook his head. He kept staring at the musicians. The music was haunting. It was amazing to have been invited in by the ghosts.

"What year is this?" Mitch asked.

"You mean, when this dance really took place?" Barry replied.

"Yeah."

Barry shrugged. "The graves around the chapel are from the mid-1800s," he said. "So, my guess is around then."

The music was clear and lively. Mitch wasn't imagining it.

"Seems like it's real tonight," he said.

"It is," Barry said. "It was real back then. And it's real right now."

They danced one more time with the women. All of the ghosts seemed to be having great fun. They laughed and sang and danced with energy.

This is a good night for them to be stuck on, Mitch thought.

When they finally left the chapel, Mitch and Barry laughed all the way down the hill. Barry headed for home. Mitch walked along the dark streets of Marshfield.

What a night, he thought. *A real dance with a real girl. A kiss on his hand and maybe a little bite. A scary but exciting dance with ghosts!* This was a Halloween he'd never forget.

A flashing red light caught his eye. It was over on Brook Street. That was where Mercy lived.

Mitch turned the corner. His heart sank. There were two police cars in front of Mercy's house. All of the downstairs lights were on.

This didn't look good at all.

Mitch took off running again.

Uh-oh, he thought as got near his own house. The lights were on there, too. His parents must be awake.

They opened the door before he even got to it.

"Where have you been?" his father asked.

"Out with Barry," Mitch replied.

"It's one o'clock in the morning!" his mother said. "You were supposed to be home hours ago."

"I was," Mitch said. "But then we went back out. It's Halloween. Midnight on Halloween is the coolest time."

"Get in here," his father said. "You know better than this."

They all sat at the kitchen table.

"What's the story?" his mother asked.

"No story," Mitch said. "We were just having fun. I didn't know it was so late."

His father cleared his throat. "Neither did we. Until we got a phone call that woke us up."

"A young girl named Mercy called a little while ago," said his mom. "She was very upset. Imagine how surprised we were when you weren't here."

"Sorry about that," Mitch said. "I lost track of time."

"She left a number," said his mom. "She asked that you call her when you got home. No matter what time it is."

"Is it okay if I do?"

Mitch's dad looked at his mom. "I suppose so," he said, "since she was so upset. But make it quick. And then get to bed."

His parents stood up.

"One more thing," his dad said. "Brush your teeth and use some mouthwash. Your breath smells horrible!"

Mitch grabbed the phone and walked to the den. He shut the door.

Mercy answered the phone.

"Are you okay?" Mitch asked.

She sounded as if she'd been crying. "The police were here."

"I know," Mitch said. "I saw the cars."

"You did?"

"Yeah. A few minutes ago. What happened?"

"They were talking to my father. Something about the stolen blood. I didn't hear everything. But it was scary."

"I'm sorry."

"Where were you?" Mercy asked. "Didn't you go home after you left me?"

"I stayed out a little while," Mitch said. "Are you all right?"

Mercy sniffed. "No. I'm scared."

"Are the cops still there?"

"No."

"Did they arrest your father?"

"No," Mercy said. "He's here. But they said they might be back."

Mitch let out his breath. "I wish I could

help."

Mercy sniffed again, harder. "Will you meet me somewhere?"

"Now?" Mitch thought for a few seconds. "My parents would never let me go back out. I was much too late getting in just now."

"There's no way I can sleep," Mercy said. "Would you meet me in the morning?"

"Sure. As early as you want."

"Six o'clock?"

"Sure," Mitch said. "I'll meet you on the corner of Brook Street."

"Thanks."

"I have to go now. Don't worry, Mercy."

"I'll try not to. But I will."

Mitch was thirsty. His mouth tasted worse than ever. He got a large glass of orange juice and went back to the den.

Mitch's Notes: Saturday, November 1. 1:24 a.m.

The cops know. They must still be looking

for evidence. Otherwise they would have arrested Mercy's father. Stolen blood! And from a blood drive. That's pretty bad. He must have really needed it.

How much does Mercy know? Could she not even realize that her parents are vampires? Or that she might be, too? Can vampires be as nice as she is? Can they be harmless? Or do they just get worse as time goes on? Will she become a blood-thirsty ghoul, too? Or can she stay the way she is?

Mitch went to his room. He sat on his bed for a long time. He didn't want to sleep. He couldn't have slept anyway. Too many things were churning around in his head.

He was worried about Mercy. He hoped that she wouldn't change.

Because I don't want to be stuck, he thought. *Like a ghost. Remembering this one good day forever. Or one bad one.*

Chapter 11:
A New Day

It was still very dark when Mitch opened his eyes. He'd slept for a couple of hours. His watch said five twenty-one. His mouth tasted like a swamp.

He brushed his teeth again. He gargled with mouthwash for two minutes. Then he put his sweatshirt and jacket back on and went out.

Mitch walked through Evergreen Cemetery. It was all quiet now. No one else was out. The backstreets were empty, too.

There were smashed pumpkins here and there in the street. Somebody had spilled red and orange candies on the sidewalk. A cardboard skeleton had blown down from someone's porch.

Mitch walked to Marshfield Grove. He wanted to get another look at the chapel. Then he'd go back to meet Mercy.

The grass in the cemetery was wet with dew. He couldn't see very far because of the fog. Some birds were chirping. But the sun wouldn't rise for at least another hour.

The chapel was quiet and dark. No one would ever guess that there had been a big party there a few hours before. A ghost party!

Mitch peeked through a hole in a board. Then he tried the door. It was bolted shut. It always was.

He took out his flashlight and shined it on some gravestones. They were from the

1850s and 1860s. Were these the dancers from last night? He'd never know for sure.

Had that dance really taken place so many years ago? Or did the ghosts get together every Halloween night for a new party?

Mitch yawned. He was glad it was Saturday. He could nap later if he needed to. He sat on the steps of the chapel. The sky was as dark as the middle of the night. He leaned against the cold stones and shut his eyes.

When he checked his watch it said five forty-eight. Mercy would probably show up early. He walked down the grassy hill toward the street.

Mercy was waiting on the corner. She was wearing a black jacket with the hood up. She gave a small smile as Mitch walked over. That necklace with the blue stone was still around her neck.

Mitch leaned close. "How are you?" he

asked.

Mercy backed away. She wrinkled her nose. "Do you want a mint?"

"No, thanks."

"Believe me," Mercy said, "you want one."

"Oh, yeah." He'd forgotten about his garlic breath. "My mouth smells pretty bad, huh?"

"Worse than bad," Mercy said. She handed him a roll of mints. "You'd better keep these. What did you eat?"

"Garlic."

"Why?"

Mitch looked at the ground. He put two mints in his mouth.

"Because of me?" Mercy asked.

Mitch sighed. "Just to be sure," he said.

"To keep me away?"

"No!" Mitch reached out and gripped Mercy's arm gently. "Not at all. I don't want you to stay away from me."

"Then why?"

Mitch pointed to the back of his hand. The mark was gone now. "When you bit me," he said, "I was afraid I might get infected."

"Infected by what?" Mercy had tears in her eyes again.

"I just wanted to make sure."

"I'm not a vampire," she said softly.

"I know."

"No, you don't," she said. She looked away.

"You did bite my hand," Mitch said.

"I kissed it first," Mercy said.

"I know. That was nice."

"I'd never hurt you, Mitch."

"I wouldn't hurt you either."

Mercy put her head down and rested it against Mitch's chest. "I was so scared last night," she said.

"Tell me about it," Mitch said. He motioned for her to walk with him. "Come on."

They didn't say anything for a few minutes. Mitch led her toward Main Street. They could sit on a bench and talk.

A few cars were moving on Main Street. A handful of people were out, too.

"It's kind of cold," Mercy said. "Can we go inside somewhere?"

Mitch looked around. The coffee shop had just opened. Already a few people were inside.

"We could sit in there," he said.

They sat at a table near the window. "We should get something," Mercy said. "We can't just sit here."

Mitch reached into his pocket. He had his wallet. "What do you want?" he asked.

"You should get some tea," Mercy said. "Peppermint and ginger. It will take away some of that bad breath."

They went up to the counter to order. Mercy got tea, too. And they decided to split a blueberry muffin. It was warm from the oven.

"The cops weren't mean," Mercy said after they sat down again. "But they were firm. Someone told them that my dad might have stolen the blood from the Red Cross."

Mitch took a sip of the tea. It was boiling hot, but it smelled good. He put down the cup.

"Do they have any evidence?" Mitch asked.

"They said they have some. They tried to get him to confess. But he wouldn't."

Mercy put her hands over her eyes. Mitch could tell that she was crying. He touched her wrist. She put down her hands and blew her nose on a napkin.

"Have some of the muffin," Mitch said.

Mercy broke off a piece and put it into her mouth. Mitch took some, too. He looked at a poster on the wall. It said that there would be a guitar player performing that night.

"My father didn't say much to them," Mercy said. "He just said yes or no when they asked questions."

"Did he seem worried?"

"Hard to tell," Mercy said. "I couldn't see him. I was sitting in the dark at the top of the stairs. Nobody knew I was listening."

"How long were they there?" Mitch asked.

"The police? About half an hour. But they told my dad not to leave town today."

Mitch let out a low whistle. He put both hands around his teacup, which was still very warm.

Mercy turned her head when Mitch whistled. She winced.

Mitch put his hand over his mouth. "Still bad?"

"Drink some tea."

Mitch put another mint in his mouth. He

sipped the tea. It burned his tongue a little.

Several people had come in to get coffee. They were waiting in line. As one man got his cup, he headed straight for the door and to his car.

"Big hurry," Mitch said.

"Adults rush through life," Mercy said.

Mitch took another piece of the muffin. This one had a big, whole blueberry in it. He held it out for Mercy. She took it from him and smiled.

"I had a great time last night," she said. "I mean, before the police and all."

Mitch nodded. "It was fun. Thanks for talking me into it."

"No problem. You were a good dancer."

"I was?"

Mercy laughed. "For it being your first time."

Mitch laughed, too. "I didn't think there ever would be a first time."

Mercy took a drink from her cup. "So,

what did you do after you left me last night?"

"Went back to one of the cemeteries," Mitch said. "I saw some more ghosts. Did you sleep at all?"

Mercy shook her head. "I was too worried about my dad. Would he really steal blood? And what's going to happen if he did? Will he go to jail?"

"I doubt it," Mitch said. "People do much worse stuff than that and go free."

"I suppose." She picked up a muffin crumb and squeezed it between her thumb and first finger. Then she looked at her nails. They were shiny. Probably with a clear polish.

Mitch took a bigger gulp of the tea. It was still hot, but not too hot. He felt a tingle in his throat as it went down. Very minty. *That should help,* he thought.

"This is a great town," Mercy said.

"Yeah, it is."

"I hope we can stay," she said.

Mercy tapped on the table with her fingertips. "When's the next dance?" she asked.

"Probably not until Valentine's Day," Mitch said.

"That's a long time." Mercy pointed to the poster for the guitar player's show. "Do they allow kids at those things?"

"I don't see why not," Mitch said.

Mercy finally smiled again. "Want to go?"

"Sure," Mitch said. "Eight o'clock."

"I'd better get some sleep this afternoon."

"Me too."

Mercy took a bigger piece of the muffin. "This is really tasty."

"We can get another one."

"Okay."

Mitch went to the counter again. He had to wait behind a woman who was getting six coffees to go. He kept looking over at Mercy.

"Think he'll be any good?" Mercy asked when Mitch came back with the muffin.

"Who?"

Mercy pointed to the poster. "That guy. Pete Johnson."

Mitch looked at the poster again. Original songs and covers. Light rock. Folk. Country.

"I guess he's good enough to play here," Mitch said. "It takes guts to do that. Even if he isn't any good."

"Like dancing."

Mitch grinned. "Yeah. Like dancing."

"Do you play anything?" Mercy asked.

Mitch shook his head. "My parents made me take piano lessons in second grade. I was bad."

"How bad?"

"Worse than my breath."

Mercy let out a big laugh. "I played the flute for a while."

Mitch thought about the ghostly flute

player last night. That music had been beautiful. "You gave it up?"

"I got into other things," Mercy said. "Soccer. Painting."

"Oh."

"The trouble is, we move around so much that I can't ever stick with a soccer team," she said.

"How often do you move?"

"I've been in six different schools," she said. "I started at one in September. Wasn't there even two months before we came here."

"That's tough."

"Yeah," Mercy said. She looked right into Mitch's eyes and smiled. "But in this case, I'm really glad we moved."

"Me too."

"I'm just worried that we'll have to do it all over again," she said. "If my dad's in trouble."

"Has anything like this ever happened

before?"

Mercy shrugged. "Not that I know about." She finished her tea. "But we've had to move in a hurry sometimes. Like I said."

Mitch nodded. He looked at his watch. It was nearly seven o'clock. His parents would be up. But there was nothing wrong with being out too early!

Mercy yawned.

"Ready to go?" Mitch asked.

"Yeah. I think I'll be able to sleep. Things seem less weird during the day."

"Right. Let's go."

She pointed to the poster again. "Eight o'clock."

"Can't wait," Mitch said. "Let's meet here at seven forty-five."

"Sounds great."

He'd made her feel better. That was one of the best things he'd ever done.

Chapter 12:
A Good Night Ends Badly

Mitch's Notes: Saturday, November 1.   7:36 a.m.

Wow.   I've never had such a close friend who was a girl.   She might be the best friend I've ever had.   Even if she did bite my hand last night!

Mitch went back to bed and slept until noon.   His stomach was growling with hunger when he woke up.   He ate a carton of yogurt, two apples, a leftover chicken leg, and two spoonfuls of peanut butter right out of the jar.

Jared and Stan wanted to get together to play basketball. But Mitch was still tired. He watched a football game on TV. Then he went back to the computer.

Barry sent him an instant message. He asked if Mitch had heard anything about Mercy's father.

Mitch: Like what?
Barry: I don't know. Anything.

Why would he be asking about that? Mitch wondered. That all had happened after Barry had left for the night.

Mitch thought for a moment. Then he typed a response.

Mitch: I haven't heard a thing.
Barry: Me either. Just remember, Mitch. Vampires are not your friends!

Mitch stared at the computer screen. He

tried to think of something else to write. But he didn't feel like chatting with Barry. He logged off and went to his room.

He slept for another hour. He felt great when he woke up. He took a short run in the cemetery. Then he showered and ate dinner.

Mitch's Notes: Saturday, November 1. 6:40 p.m.

My energy is back. Tonight should be fun. I don't care what Barry says. Vampires can be great friends!

An hour later, Mitch sat on the steps of the coffee house and watched the traffic go by. The guitar player was setting up in a corner of the shop. It was just him and his guitar.

When Mitch saw Mercy walking toward him, he jumped up. He walked toward her quickly.

She was grinning. She put her face right

up to his.

"Much better," she said. "One more cup of peppermint tea should do it."

"Sounds good," Mitch said.

"I'll buy it this time."

There were nine people listening to the concert. He was a good guitar player, but his voice was kind of rough. Mercy and Mitch each had a cup of tea and a bag of potato chips. When the guitarist took a break, they went outside.

"Nice night," Mercy said. The sky had cleared. They could see a lot of stars overhead.

"Want to walk?" Mitch asked.

"Yes."

They looked in store windows. Then they checked the posters at the movie theater to see what would be playing soon.

Mercy nodded her head back toward the coffee shop. "Would you ever want to do something like that?"

"Like what?" Mitch asked.

"Sing and play guitar," she said. "In front of a crowd. Be a star."

"Stars get more than nine people to watch," Mitch said with a grin.

"You know what I mean," Mercy said.

"Like I said before, it takes guts."

"You have guts."

Mitch laughed. "You need guts and talent."

Mercy laughed, too. "At least you have one out of two."

"Guts and no talent," Mitch said. "That's a dangerous combination."

There were several restaurants on Main Street. So, the sidewalk was busy. Once when Mitch looked back, he saw Barry and Jared about a block behind them.

"Let's go in here," Mitch said, pointing to a small store. He wanted to avoid Barry.

But when they came out, Barry and Jared were still a half of a block away. They started walking when Mitch and Mercy did.

Mitch could tell that Mercy hadn't seen them. *Why are they following us?* he wondered. *Just to be a pain, probably.*

"What do you want to do?" Mitch asked.

"I'm having fun just hanging out," Mercy said. "We don't have to do anything."

"We could go see the end of the concert," Mitch said.

They turned to walk back. Mitch saw Barry and Jared dart into an alley.

There were eleven people in the coffee shop now. It was loud enough that they could hear it from outside.

"Let's stay here," Mercy said.

"On the sidewalk?"

"Why not?" Mercy took a few dance steps. "Remember?" she said. "Out, out. In, in."

Mitch blushed. It was one thing to dance at school. Especially when he was wearing a gorilla mask. But in public? Not a chance.

Mercy kept dancing. She gave Mitch a big smile. He moved his shoulders a little. But he didn't try to do the footwork.

When the song ended, Mercy sat on the steps. "Not enough guts?" she asked.

Mitch laughed. "I guess not." He sat next to her.

"I understand," she said. "Even I feel a little funny about dancing on the sidewalk."

Mercy leaned back and rested her elbows on the steps. She closed her eyes and listened to the music.

Mitch saw Barry peeking around the corner of the building. Mitch held up his hands as if to say, "What are you doing?"

Barry ducked out of sight again.

Mercy opened her eyes. She looked at Mitch's raised hands. "What's going on?" she asked.

"Just keeping time to the music," Mitch

said. He swayed his arms.

"Great moves," Mercy teased. "You'll be a star after all."

The show ended soon after that. Then, they moved to a bench across the street.

"I need to get home soon," Mercy said.

"Me too," Mitch said. "Last night was a late one."

"What about tomorrow?" Mercy asked. "Do you have any plans?"

"Nothing special," Mitch said.

"We could go for a run," Mercy said.

"Sure. Let's do that. Then we can kick around a soccer ball."

"That would be fun," Mercy said. "Could we get a game together? Would your friends play?"

"Probably," Mitch said. "I'll round up some people."

Mercy yawned. "I'm way behind on sleep," she said.

"Me too." Mitch stood up and held out his hand.

They laughed about the dance on the walk to Mercy's house. Stan had danced a lot worse than Mitch.

"He didn't have a good coach like I did," Mitch said. He stopped walking and did a few dance steps. "Out, out. In, in."

Mercy clapped. But then she let out a gasp. "What's that?" she said.

Red lights were flashing on Brook Street. Mitch could see the police cars.

"This is a nightmare," Mercy said. Her mouth hung open as she stared at the cars. She walked very quickly toward the house.

The front door opened. Mrs. Knight stepped onto the porch. "Mercy," she called, "you need to get in here."

Mercy turned to Mitch. "I'll call you." Mercy ran the few steps to the porch.

Mitch waited for a few minutes. Then he slowly walked home.

Another great evening was ending badly.

Chapter 13:
Fleeing

This is so weird. How can such a nice girl have a father who keeps getting into trouble? I need to sleep, but I can't. Mercy hasn't called me, so maybe things are okay. But maybe they're worse than ever. The cops wouldn't have come back unless they had a good reason to.

Mitch walked slowly up the stairs. He stretched out on his bed and stared at the ceiling in the dark. He didn't want to sleep. He nodded off a few times, but each time he woke up sweating. He was breathing hard, too.

He dreamed that a pack of wolves had him surrounded in the cemetery. They were closing in and woofing. And each one had sharp, shiny fangs.

All night he tossed and turned. He had terrible dreams. He never slept for more than twenty minutes at a time.

The phone rang before six a.m. Mitch knew who it was. He ran down the stairs to answer it.

"Hi," he said. "What's going on?"

"I have to see you right away," Mercy said. "Can you meet me at my house?"

"Okay. What happened?"

"I'll tell you when you get here," she said. "Please hurry. I don't have much time."

Mitch got dressed and ran all the way. The streets were dark and empty. Mercy met him on the corner. They walked toward

Evergreen Cemetery.

"They took my dad away in handcuffs," Mercy said.

"Wow."

"He's in big trouble," she said. "They said the police were looking for him back in New Jersey, too. And in Ohio."

"Ohio?"

"That's where we were last summer." Mercy stopped walking and sat on the curb. She put her face in her hands and cried.

Mitch sat next to her. He put his hand on her back. She was shaking. So was he.

"Is he in jail?" Mitch asked.

Mercy shook her head hard. "No." She wiped her nose with the back of her hand. "My mom bailed him out."

"What a mess."

"I was alone for most of the night," Mercy said. "They kept him at the courthouse for hours."

"You should have called me."

"My mom said I couldn't use the phone," Mercy said. "In case she had to get in touch with me. I was so scared."

"I'm so sorry."

Mercy took a deep breath and leaned into Mitch. "He's due back in court on Monday."

"That's too bad."

"I know. It's why we're leaving."

"You're leaving?"

Mercy started crying harder. She couldn't talk. She just nodded and looked at the ground.

"He's not going to court?" Mitch asked.

Mercy shook her head. "We're fleeing. Just like every time before."

"There were other times?"

Mercy sniffed. "Yeah."

"They'll catch him again."

"I know." Mercy sobbed. Mitch patted her shoulder.

"Will you be back?" he asked. He felt

like crying, too.

"How can we?" Mercy said. "They'll put him in jail for good if they catch him again."

They didn't say anything for a few minutes. Mitch's thoughts were spinning. *Mercy was leaving? Right now?*

"Can they prove he stole the blood?" he finally asked.

"I don't know." Mercy looked up at him. "I don't need proof. I know he did it. I saw the bottles. I was just fooling myself into thinking they were filled with juice."

"I won't see you again?" Mitch couldn't believe this was happening.

Mercy sobbed and shook her head. "I have to go. They're packing the car right now."

Mitch wiped his eyes. "I'll walk with you," he said.

"Let's just stay here for another minute," Mercy said. She grabbed Mitch's hand and

held tight. Then she took off her necklace
and put it in his palm. "Keep this."

Could this be real? She's leaving already,
Mitch thought. *I've hardly gotten to know
her.*

"I'll get ahold of you when we find a new
place," Mercy whispered. "I promise."

"Okay," Mitch said.

"Maybe I am a vampire," Mercy
whispered.

"You think so?"

"I don't know. My parents are. Doesn't
that make me one, too?"

"Not for sure," Mitch said.

Mercy nodded. She smiled slightly, even
though tears were running down her face.
"I never thought I was," she said. "But it's
weird. When I'm with you, I think maybe
I am."

"How come?"

"I don't know. But I did want to bite
your hand," she said. "Harder, I mean."

"Hard enough to draw blood?"

Mercy closed her mouth tight and looked at her feet. "Maybe," she whispered. "But I'd never want to hurt you."

They walked slowly back to the house. Mercy's parents were shoving boxes and suitcases into the trunk of their car. Mr. Knight kept looking around.

Three minutes later, the Knights were speeding away. Mercy waved sadly as they passed Mitch. She was crying.

Mitch stared at the house. They hadn't even shut the front door. A broken lamp sat on the porch next to the three jack-o'-lanterns.

Mitch stood in that spot for a long, long time. He squeezed the stone on the necklace.

He couldn't find the energy to move.

Chapter 14:
Good News

Mitch's Notes: Sunday, November 2. 10:33 a.m.

Will I ever hear from her again? She said I will. But they must be going far away. Even if they catch her father, Mercy couldn't come back here. Could she?

Nothing seemed real to Mitch now. He'd been so happy last evening. Hanging out on Main Street. Joking around with Mercy. Listening to music. Eating potato chips.

Now he felt like a smashed pumpkin.

Mitch stared at the computer screen for a long time. Finally an instant message appeared from Barry.

Barry: Dude. You busy?
Mitch: No.
Barry: Meet u at the bagel place?

Mitch thought about that for a minute. He didn't feel like seeing Barry. He didn't feel like seeing anybody. But his stomach was growling. So he typed OK.

Then he walked downtown in a daze. The sky had a lot of clouds. It felt like it might rain any minute.

Barry was waiting by the counter. "What kind do you want?" he asked.

Mitch shook his head. "Raisin, I guess."

Barry paid. They went to a table in the corner.

"You all right?" Barry asked.

"Why do you ask?"

Barry shrugged. "I think you had a

rough night."

"What do you know about it?" Mitch asked. "And why were you spying on us?"

Barry took a bite of his bagel. "Just looking out for you."

"Thanks," Mitch said. "But I can take care of myself."

Barry nodded. "I know."

"They left town this morning."

"I figured."

Mitch felt his face getting hot. "How did you figure that?"

"I saw the police cars."

Mitch reached across the table and poked Barry in the chest. "Did you call the cops?"

Barry looked out the window. Then he looked down at his bagel and tore it in half. "I had to. They stole the blood, Mitch. You know that."

Mitch glared at Barry. Mercy was gone because of him. But Barry was right.

They'd both seen the evidence.

"Sorry," Barry said. "I really am. I liked her. I hope she comes back to Marshfield."

"Not likely," Mitch said. He shut his eyes. His head hurt. He'd had very little sleep all weekend.

Mitch took a bite of his bagel. He chewed very slowly. He usually loved raisin bagels. This one tasted like dust.

"Did that photo turn out?" Mitch finally asked. "The one of the ghosts at the funeral?"

Barry frowned and shook his head. "That never seems to work," he said.

Barry leaned forward. He tapped on the table. "Mercy's father is a vampire, Mitch. And a criminal."

Mitch sighed and looked away. "I know." He stood up. "Thanks for the bagel," he mumbled. He headed for the door.

"See you later," Barry said.

Mitch walked over to the coffee shop.

He sat on the steps for a few minutes. Then he went to the magazine store. And the movie theater. He visited all the places he'd been with Mercy the night before. But each place he went to made him sadder.

Then he went back to Evergreen Cemetery. Lots more leaves had fallen. Many of the trees were bare. A few drops of rain came down.

Mitch climbed the steep hill. He stood by John Chase's gravestone. He reached into his pocket and took out the necklace Mercy had given him. The light-blue stone was oval. It had a few streaks of white. The strap was black and it stretched a bit. It was probably leather.

Mitch put it back in his pocket. The rain was coming down harder now. He walked down the hill and went home to write in his computer journal.

Mitch's Notes: Sunday, November 2.   11:55 a.m.

*Why didn't he just face up to things and
go to court? Why couldn't he leave Mercy
and her mom here? What good is fleeing
going to do? It only makes things worse.
I guess if he goes to jail, he won't get the
blood he needs.*

It sure makes things worse for me.

But it must be worst of all for Mercy.

Mitch's dad stuck his head into the den.
"The pre-game show starts in a minute."

"Okay," Mitch said. He always watched
a football game with his father on Sundays.
He didn't feel like it today. But what else
was he going to do? It would at least take
his mind off this other stuff.

At exactly noon an instant message came
on the screen.

MJK: Mitch?

He didn't recognize the sender. MJK.
Mercy J. Knight?
Mitch quickly typed a response.

Mitch: Is that you? Are you OK?

MJK: My mom and I are at a motel. We got stopped trying to cross the border into Canada. Dad's in jail.

Mitch didn't know how to respond to that. He wanted to say, "Great!" That was how he felt. But that wouldn't be fair to Mercy. This was her father, after all.

MJK: We're OK.

That was good news.

Mitch: I was so worried about you, Mercy. What happens now?

MJK: I don't know. He's in trouble in at least three states. My mom and I are going to my grandmother's house for a while.

Mitch: Where's that?

MJK: Back in Ohio.

Mitch: That was a long way from here. Do you think you'll ever get back to Marshfield?

MJK: I hope so. But I have no idea when.

Mitch let out a sigh of relief. He'd been

afraid he'd never hear from Mercy again. Now here she was already.

They didn't chat long. Mercy had to start the long drive.

Mitch felt a lot better already. There was hope. Mercy would be OK. Even if she lived in a different state, they could talk anytime they wanted to.

"Football!" Dad yelled.

"OK," Mitch said. He wrapped Mercy's necklace around his wrist. He held the stone loosely in his palm. He didn't know when he'd see her again. But for now, he'd remember all the fun they'd had.

Maybe she'd be back. Maybe they would dance again some night.

Identifying Vampires
from Mitch Morris

Step 1: Check out the suspected vampire for the following: pale skin, dark hair and eyes, pointy teeth.

Step 2: Watch what the suspected vampire eats. If he or she avoids garlic, there is a chance he or she is a vampire.

Step 3: Look out for a person who often drinks lots of red things and calls it their "life force." He or she may be a vampire.

Step 4: Watch for biters. People don't often bite others, unless they are toddlers. If someone bites you, and tells you they wanted to bite even harder, you may be looking at a vampire.

Step 5: Keep your eyes peeled while in a cemetery. Ghosts, vampires, zombies, and ghost hunters spend time there.

Vampire Facts
from Mitch Morris

#1: Vampires have been reported for centuries. But the idea that they can't be out during the day is new. It was first suggested in a horror movie.

#2: To cure yourself of a vampire bite, hang a bag of salt around your neck.

#3: Vampires drink blood to absorb the strength of their victims.

#4: Bitten victims don't always turn into vampires.

#5: Garlic will keep vampires away . . . mostly because you smell like garlic.

#6: Not all vampires are evil or out to drink human blood. Some are just like everyone else.

#7: Some vampires can bewitch people and get them to do whatever they want. It helps if the vampire is pretty.

#8: Vampires can be nice, funny, smart, and generous. Get to know them before you judge them.

ABOUT THE ...

Author

Baron Specter is the pen name of Rich Wallace, who has written many novels for kids and teenagers. His latest books include the Kickers soccer series and the novel *Sports Camp*.

Illustrator

Setch Kneupper has years of experience thinking he saw a ghost, although Graveyard Diaries is the first series of books he's illustrated about the ordeal.